Show Us Where You Live,
HUMPBACK

by **BERYL YOUNG**

illustrated by **SAKIKA KIKUCHI**

GREYSTONE KIDS

GREYSTONE BOOKS • VANCOUVER/BERKELEY

Show us where you live, Humpback,
in the warm waters of this southern bay.
We see you now with your newborn calf.
Here she will grow and learn.

She floats close by you,
a small shadow in this new world.
You glide together through the sparkling sea.

Your flippers sway like gentle curtains,
keeping your young one safe.

This is where I live,
 my home, where I learn and grow,
where I am safe.

You are a giant riding the waves, Humpback,
as big as a school bus.
Your calf is hungry, and once again
she takes your milk, not a drop wasted.

Every day she grows and grows.
One day she will be as big as you.

I am growing too,
getting big, bigger.
See how tall I am!

Show your calf the ways of the sea, Humpback.
    Teach her how to swim.
Guide her with your tail fluke
    so she learns the drifts and sways of the tides.

As she grows stronger, you swim faster,
    but always, she stays close.

She looks into your eye
and sees herself.

Every day I learn new things.
I can pump my own swing.
Watch me, Mama!

Let us see you splash, Humpback.
Your calf watches too.
Your mighty flippers
slap the water hard.
Your tail beats and crashes,
smacks and splashes,
sending rolling waves across the sea.

Whack your fin! Thwap your fluke!
You are loud! You're a wonder!

I make smashes and splashes.
Water tickles my nose.
I blink my eyes and laugh.

Surprise us when you blow, Humpback.
Look! A plume shoots up from your blowhole,

a jet of sparkling bubbles.

We wait for one more.

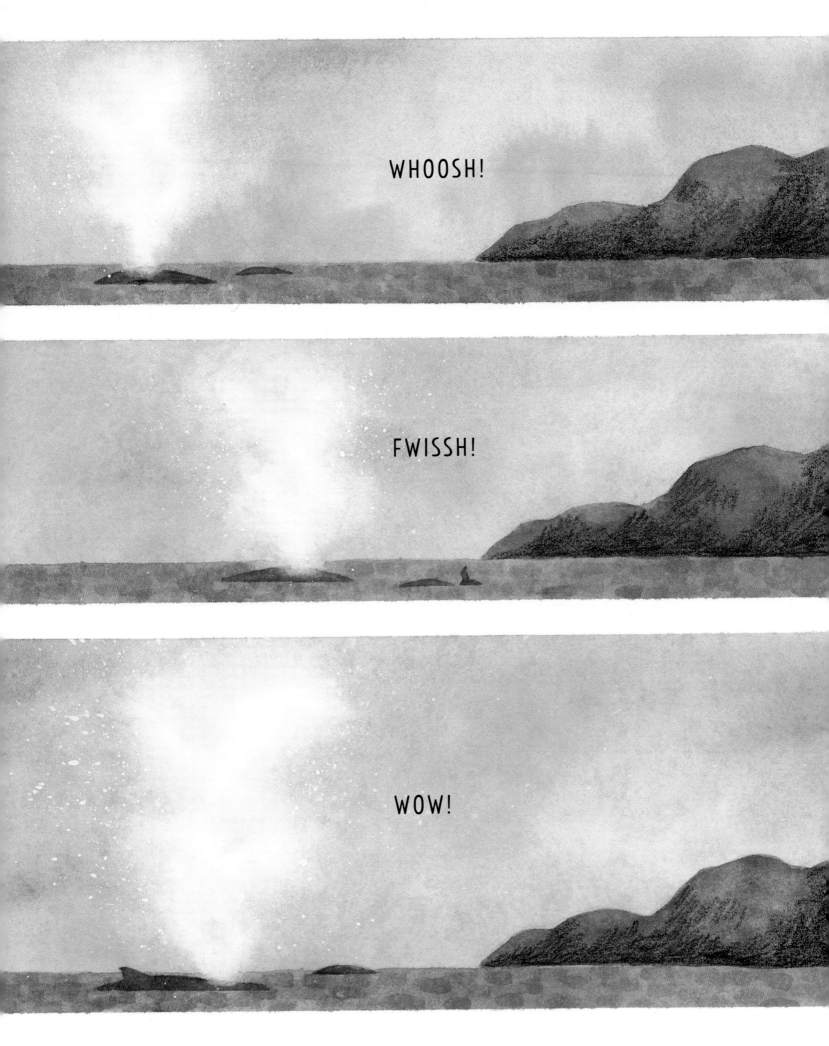

I can puff. I can blow.

WHOOSH!

I can make bubbles too.

Up,
up,
zoom up!
Water sprays
from your wings.
Soaring into the air
you are a seabird,
and with a strong leap
suddenly you breach high.
We watch for you in the water.
We wait to see you jump,
Humpback.

Up!
Up!

I can jump in the air.
Higher and higher!

We hear singing, Humpback.
Another whale calls with new songs,
siren notes that shrill and curl,
curl and shrill
in a chorus of silver sonnets.

I can sing.

I can shout too.

Everyone can hear me!

Show us how your calf sleeps, Humpback,
how she floats close beside you.
Your steady flipper pillows her,
keeping her safe
as you float deeper into the dark.

Then still sleeping,
   you rise together to breathe
     and gently lower again.

I rest against my mother's side.
She sings to me.
I close my eyes and sleep.

We have seen where you live, Humpback,
   your calf by your side
      in the warm waters of this southern bay.

Now we will drift and dream
of the wide sea and the whales
in this wondrous world we share.

ABOUT HUMPBACK WHALES

Humpbacks are wonderful whales. It's an unforgettable experience to watch them leap powerfully into the air with their long flippers out like wings. The skin of their heads is covered in big knobs like the bumps on dill pickles, and their wide mouths look as if the whales are smiling at us.

Humpbacks are marine mammals, and like all mammals they are warm-blooded, feed their babies milk, and need to breathe air.

An adult humpback whale can be as big and as heavy as five elephants! They can live for fifty years, traveling with grace around the seas of the world.

The cycle of the humpback's life starts when the calves grow for eleven months inside female humpbacks while the adult whales feed in the cold waters near the north and south poles. When it is time, the whales migrate, traveling day and night as far as five thousand miles to warm tropical waters. Here their calves are born.

A newborn whale is not small like a human baby.
A calf is about the size of a compact car and grows
quickly, doubling its weight in two weeks. The
months go by until the time comes to leave the
warm bays. Now the young whale is strong enough
to swim beside its mother for the return journey to
colder waters.

Female whales give birth every two or three years,
and so the cycle of the wonderful humpback whales
begins again.

21 22 23 24 25 5 4 3 2 1

Greystone Kids / Greystone Books Ltd.
greystonebooks.com

Cataloguing data available from Library and Archives Canada
ISBN 978-1-77164-573-7 (cloth)
ISBN 978-1-77164-574-4 (epub)

MIX
Paper from
responsible sources
FSC® C012700
FSC
www.fsc.org

Editing by Kallie George
Copy editing by Antonia Banyard
Proofreading by Doeun Rivendell
Jacket and interior design by Sara Gillingham Studio
The illustrations in this book were rendered in watercolor.

The author wishes to thank Dr. Andrew Trites, Director of the Marine Mammal Research Unit,
Institute for the Oceans and Fisheries, UBC.

Printed and bound in Malaysia on ancient-forest-friendly paper by Tien Wah Press.

Greystone Books gratefully acknowledges the Musqueam, Squamish, and Tsleil-Waututh
peoples on whose land our office is located.

Greystone Books thanks the Canada Council for the Arts, the British Columbia Arts Council,
the Province of British Columbia through the Book Publishing Tax Credit, and the
Government of Canada for supporting our publishing activities.

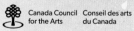